THE MOTHER GOOSE LIBRARY

See-saw, sacradown,
Which is the way to London town?
One foot up and the other foot down,
That is the way to London town.
And just the same, over dale and hill,
Is also the way to wherever you will.

See-saw, Jack in the hedge,
Which is the way to London Bridge?
Put on your shoes and away you trudge,
That is the way to London Bridge!

London Bridge Is Falling Down!

illustrated by Peter Spier

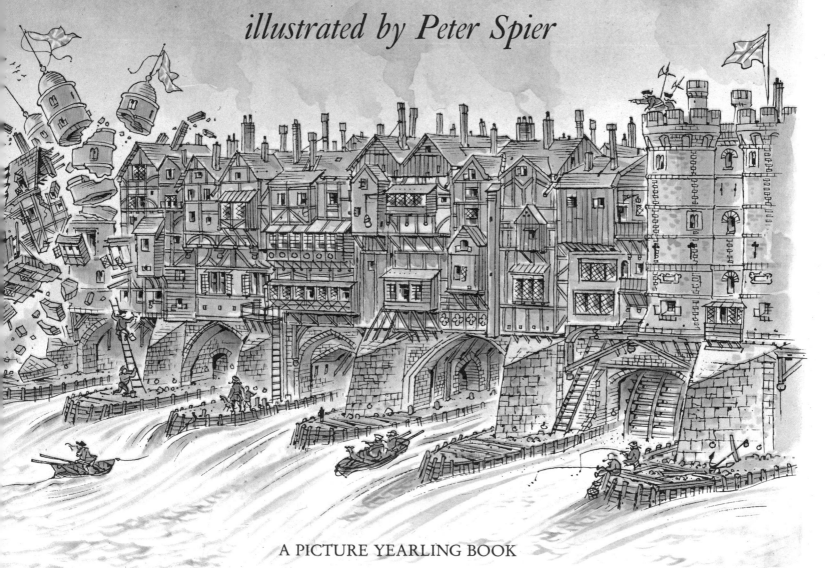

A PICTURE YEARLING BOOK

This one is for Tom!

Published by
Dell Publishing
a division of
Bantam Doubleday Dell Publishing Group, Inc.
666 Fifth Avenue
New York, New York 10103

The trademark Yearling® is registered in the U.S. Patent and
Trademark Office.

The trademark Dell® is registered in the U.S. Patent and
Trademark Office.

ISBN: 0-440-40710-9

Reprinted by arrangement with Delacorte Press, on behalf of
Doubleday

Printed in the United States of America
October 1992
10 9 8 7 6 5 4 3 2 1

London Bridge Is Falling Down!

London Bridge is falling down, falling down, falling down,

London Bridge is falling down, My fair lady.

How shall we build it up again?
Up again, up again,
How shall we build it up again?
My fair lady.

Build it up with wood and clay, wood and clay, wood and clay,

Build it up with wood and clay, My fair lady.

Wood and clay will wash away,
wash away, wash away,
Wood and clay will wash away,
My fair lady.

Build it up with iron and steel, iron and steel, iron and steel,

Build it up with iron and steel, My fair lady.

Iron and steel will bend and bow,
bend and bow, bend and bow,
Iron and steel will bend and bow,
My fair lady.

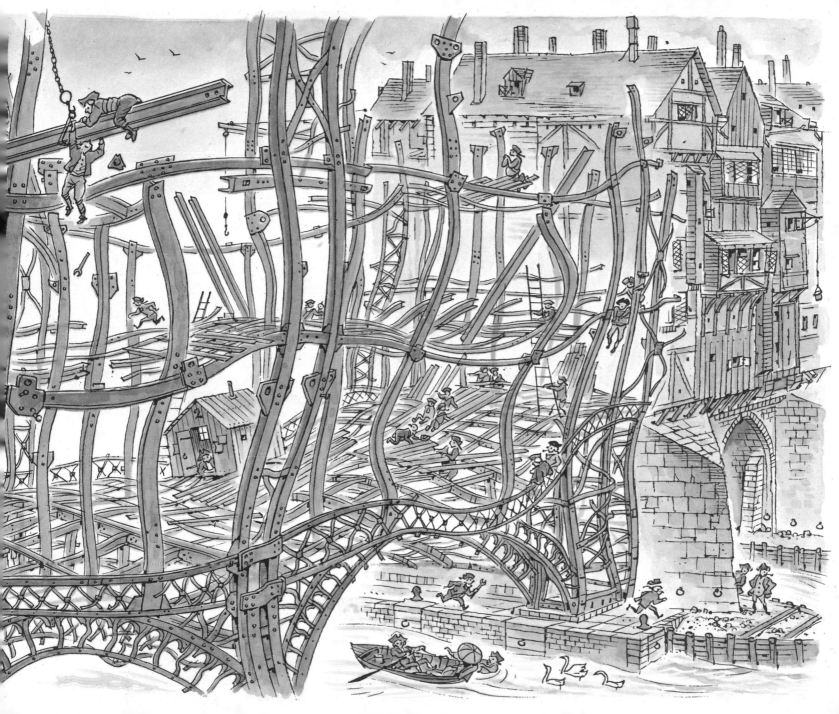

Build it up with gravel and stone, gravel and stone, gravel and stone,

Build it up with gravel and stone, My fair lady.

Gravel and stone will fall away,
fall away, fall away,
Gravel and stone will fall away,
My fair lady.

Build it up with silver and gold, silver and gold, silver and gold,

Build it up with silver and gold, My fair lady.

Silver and gold will be stolen away,
stolen away, stolen away,
Silver and gold will be stolen away,
My fair lady.

Then we must set a man to watch,
man to watch, man to watch,
Then we must set a man to watch,
My fair lady.

Suppose the man should fall asleep,
fall asleep, fall asleep,
Suppose the man should fall asleep,
My fair lady.

Give him a pipe to smoke all night,
smoke all night, smoke all night,
Give him a pipe to smoke all night,
My fair lady.

Suppose the pipe should fall and break,
fall and break, fall and break,
Suppose the pipe should fall and break,
My fair lady.

Then we will set a dog to watch,
dog to watch, dog to watch,
Then we will set a dog to watch,
My fair lady.

Suppose the dog should run away,
run away, run away,
Suppose the dog should run away,
My fair lady.

Then we shall chain him to a post,
to a post, to a post,
Then we shall chain him to a post,
My fair lady.

London Bridge is falling down,
falling down, falling down,
London Bridge is falling down,
My fair lady.

When New London Bridge was completed in 1831, the Old Bridge was finally torn down after having been in continuous use for 622 years.

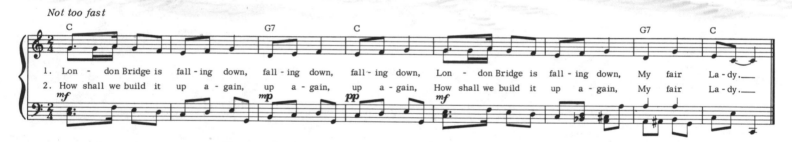

Not too fast

1. Lon - don Bridge is fall - ing down, fall - ing down, fall - ing down, Lon - don Bridge is fall - ing down, My fair La - dy.
2. How shall we build it up a - gain, up a - gain, up a - gain, How shall we build it up a - gain, My fair La - dy.

3. Build it up with wood and clay, etc.

4. Wood and clay will wash away, etc.

5. Build it up with iron and steel, etc.

6. Iron and steel will bend and bow, etc.

7. Build it up with gravel and stone, etc.

8. Gravel and stone will fall away, etc.

9. Build it up with silver and gold, etc.

10. Silver and gold will be stolen away, etc.

11. Then we must set a man to watch, etc.

12. Suppose the man should fall asleep, etc.

13. Give him a pipe to smoke all night, etc.

14. Suppose the pipe should fall and break, etc.

15. Then we will set a dog to watch, etc.

16. Suppose the dog should run away, etc.

17. Then we shall chain him to a post, etc.

18. London Bridge is falling down, etc.

LONDON BRIDGE THROUGH THE CENTURIES

Not long after their arrival in Britain in 43 B.C., so tradition says, the Romans improved the Dover road by building the first London Bridge, a wooden one, across the Thames. During the thousand years which followed, the few records which survive tell us that the Bridge was damaged or destroyed by flood, by fire, by war, and built up again many times.

In 1014, for example, the Danes took London from King Ethelred the Unready and fortified the Bridge; but the fleet of Ethelred's ally, Olaf of Norway, drove the Danes out by slinging cables around the Bridge's piers, rowing downstream with all their might, and pulling down the Bridge. The Bridge was built up again, only to be destroyed and rebuilt in 1077, 1086, and 1092. The chronicler Fitzstephen recorded a burning of the Bridge in 1136, and in 1163 Peter, bridgemaster and chaplain of St. Mary Colechurch, rebuilt the Bridge with elmwood.

In 1176, just one year before work was started on an-other famous bridge at Avignon, Peter de Colechurch began to build the first stone Bridge. Peter died before his work was complete, and he was buried in the chapel on the Bridge in 1205. At last in 1209 the Bridge was finished.

It was a wondrous feat of engineering, over three hundred yards long and twenty feet wide, supported more than thirty feet above low tide by twenty Gothic arches. There was a wooden drawbridge to let ships pass and also to seal off the Bridge against invaders. The bases of the piers on which the arches rested were protected by boat-shaped islands called starlings, which held back the tidal ebb and flow in the river so that when the tide turned there was a fall of water of about five feet. These falls turned water wheels which, at first, only ground grain, but later on, in 1580, first one and then two water wheels at the north end of the Bridge pumped water up into the City. During the winter the starlings often so slowed the flow of the river that it froze, and carnivals were held on the ice.

When the Bridge was finished in 1209, great fortress-like gateways were built at both ends, and in the same year, the first houses appeared, built partly on the Bridge and partly cantilevered out from it. Before long the Bridge was completely filled with houses and shops on both sides, and the twenty foot roadway had shrunk to twelve feet.

A toll was charged for passage over the Bridge, and these tolls not only paid for the upkeep of the Bridge but also provided a tidy income for the City of London for several years. Then Henry III took the Bridge away from the City and diverted the revenues to his own treasury. Now there were few funds available for repair of the Bridge, and during the winter of 1282 ice floes knocked down five weakened arches and the houses over them.

The Bridge played so important a part in London's life that some commentators called the City "the parasite of the Bridge." In 1216 Louis of France led his armies across the Bridge to help the English nobility in their struggle with King John. In 1304 began the grisly practice of impaling the heads of traitors on the gates of the Bridge, where 350 years later was placed the head of Oliver Cromwell. After the Battle of Poitiers in 1357, the Black Prince brought his army home in triumph over the Bridge; one observer noted that there were 128 shops on the Bridge that day, and their signs added color and gaiety to the scene. Wat Tyler led his peasant followers over the Bridge and into the City in 1381. Henry V marched victoriously over the Bridge in 1415 after the Battle of Agincourt. In 1437, we read, one Margery Bacheler left her gold wedding band to the Bridge in her will. Hans Holbein lived in a house on the Bridge from 1526 to 1528, as Hogarth was to do some 175 years later. In 1554 it was noted that the Princess Elizabeth went "thorowe London Bridge at 3 of the clock in the afternoone...." Shakespeare lived most of his life on the northern side of the Bridge and must have crossed it regularly on his way to the Globe Theatre in Southwark. In Southwark, too, were many inns, and at least part of one of them, the "George," stands there today.

In Elizabethan times the Thames around the Bridge swarmed with boats and barges, as many as three thousand of them according to one estimate, which were the taxis and delivery trucks of their time. For these boats to pass under the Bridge, through the turbulent rapids formed by the starlings, was called "shooting the Bridge." Literally

thousands of lives were lost, and many times that many boats and barges were swamped shooting the Bridge.

Fire struck the Bridge in 1623, and forty-three houses were destroyed. But in the Great London Fire of 1666 the Bridge escaped with only slight damage. Now, however, the wealthy merchants who had mainly populated the Bridge began to move away. The Bridge grew dilapidated, and in 1756 Parliament authorized it to be remodeled. By 1762 the last houses were gone from the Bridge and Peter de Colechurch's construction was hidden by new buttresses and ugly decorations. The starlings were enlarged, and shooting the Bridge became more dangerous than ever. Small wonder that Boswell recorded in 1763 that Dr. Johnson preferred to be put ashore at the old Swan steps above the Bridge and to walk down to Billingsgate wharf on the other side to rejoin his boat. Crossing over the Bridge was not entirely safe either; people were often run over by carts or wagons; holdups were everyday events.

In 1789 it was suggested that the Bridge be torn down altogether and a new one built in its place. For thirty-three years architects and planners and builders argued the project; numberless proposals and counter-proposals were brought forward and rejected. At last the House of Commons accepted Sir John Rennie's plans for the new Bridge, royal assent for it was secured, and in 1824 work began to build it up, 100 feet to the west of the old one. In 1831 the new Bridge was opened with great festivities by William IV. At the same time, demolition of the old Bridge was begun. Within a year only the starlings remained, and in a lower level of the center starling workmen uncovered the old Bridge chapel and the grave of Peter de Colechurch. When at last the site of the old Bridge was dredged, many thousands of Roman coins were found.

In 1921 excavations for the foundations of a new building near the north end of London Bridge brought to light the second arch of the old Bridge. Efforts to preserve it were unsuccessful and so, eight centuries after it was built, old London Bridge was "fallen down."

In 1962 engineers discovered that new London Bridge was beginning to fall down, too. A still newer London Bridge was completed by 1973, three arches built of concrete to carry six lanes of traffic plus forty feet of walks for pedestrians.

PETER SPIER has established himself as one of this country's most gifted children's book authors and illustrators. Among the many prestigious awards he has won are the Caldecott Medal, the Caldecott Honor Award, the *Boston Globe–Horn Book* Award, the American Book Award, and the Christopher Medal. He and his wife, Kay, live in Shoreham, New York.

THE MOTHER GOOSE LIBRARY